W9-BDO-918

Elk/Uapitíes

By JoAnn Early Macken

Reading Consultant: Jeanne Clidas, Ph.D.
Director, Roberts Wesleyan College Literacy Clinic

WEEKLY READER®
PUBLISHING

Please visit our web site at **www.garethstevens.com**.
For a free catalog describing our list of high-quality books,
call 1-877-542-2595 (USA) or 1-800-387-3178 (Canada).
Our fax: 1-877-542-2596

Library of Congress Cataloging-in-Publication Data

Macken, JoAnn Early, 1953–
      [Elk. Spanish & English]
      Elk = Uapitíes / by JoAnn Early Macken.
            p. cm. — (Animals that live in the mountains = Animales de las montañas)
      Includes bibliographical references and index.
      ISBN-10: 1-4339-2444-7   ISBN-13: 978-1-4339-2444-6 (lib. bdg.)
      ISBN-10: 1-4339-2502-8   ISBN-13: 978-1-4339-2502-3 (soft cover)
      1. Elk–Juvenile literature. I. Title. II. Title: Uapitíes.
   QL737.U55M25318   2010
   599.65'42–dc22   2009007411

This edition first published in 2010 by
Weekly Reader® Books
An Imprint of Gareth Stevens Publishing
1 Reader's Digest Road
Pleasantville, NY 10570-7000 USA

Executive Managing Editor: Lisa M. Herrington
Senior Editor: Barbara Bakowski
Cover Designers: Jennifer Ryder-Talbot and Studio Montage
Production: Studio Montage
Translators: Tatiana Acosta and Guillermo Gutiérrez
Library Consultant: Carl Harvey, Library Media Specialist, Noblesville, Indiana

Photo credits: Cover, pp. 1, 11 Shutterstock; pp. 5, 7, 9, 19 © Tom and Pat Leeson; pp. 13, 17, 21
© Michael H. Francis; p. 15 © Jeff Milton/Daybreak Imagery

Printed in the United States of America

1 2 3 4 5 6 7 8 9 14 13 12 11 10 09

Table of Contents

- - - - - - - - - - - -

Contenido

Boldface words appear in the glossary./
Las palabras en **negrita** aparecen en el glosario.

An Elk Family

A baby elk is a **calf**. A calf has white spots on its coat. The spots make the calf hard to see.

- - - - - - - - - - - - - - - - -

Una familia de uapitíes

La cría de uapití es un **cervatillo**. Su pelaje tiene manchas blancas. Las manchas hacen que el cervatillo sea difícil de ver.

calf/
cervatillo

Calves drink milk from their mothers.
In about a week, the calves can run. A few
weeks later, they start to eat grass.

- - - - - - - - - - - - - - -

Las crías beben la leche de sus madres.
En una semana, aproximadamente, los
cervatillos son capaces de correr. Unas
semanas más tarde, comienzan a
comer pasto.

Elk are larger than deer. They are smaller than moose. Like deer and moose, elk have **hooves** on their feet.

- - - - - - - - - - - - - -

Los uapitíes son más grandes que otros venados. Son más pequeños que los alces. Igual que los venados y los alces, los uapitíes tienen **pezuñas**.

hooves/
pezuñas

Life in a Herd

Elk stay in a group called a **herd**. An older female leads a herd. One elk watches for danger.

- - - - - - - - - - - - - -

La vida en la manada

Los uapitíes forman grupos llamados **manadas**. Una hembra de más edad lidera la manada. Otro uapití vigila por si hay peligro.

herd/
manada

Elk use their noses, ears, and eyes to sense danger. They see things that move. They watch out for bears and cougars.

Los uapitíes detectan el peligro con la nariz, las orejas y los ojos. Ven lo que está en movimiento. Vigilan la presencia de osos y pumas.

Elk eat grass and other plants. They swallow their food quickly. Later, they bring it up and chew it again.

- - - - - - - - - - - - - -

Los uapitíes comen pasto y otras plantas. Se tragan la comida deprisa. Más tarde, la recuperan y la vuelven a masticar.

Changing With the Seasons

Male elk have **antlers**. The antlers fall off each winter. In spring, new antlers grow.

- - - - - - - - - - - - - - -

Cambiar con las estaciones

Los machos tienen **astas**. En invierno, las astas se les caen. En primavera, las astas les vuelven a crecer.

antlers/
astas

In spring, elk move up the mountain. They look for fresh grass to eat. In fall, they move down to warmer places.

— — — — — — — — — — — — — —

Cuando llega la primavera, los uapitíes van a zonas más altas de la montaña. Allí buscan pasto fresco para comer. En el otoño, bajan a lugares más cálidos.

In winter, elk grow thick coats to keep warm. They dig through snow to find food. They may eat bark and twigs. In spring, they **molt**, or shed their thick coats.

- - - - - - - - - - - - - - - -

En el invierno, a los uapitíes les crece un denso pelaje con el que se resguardan del frío. Para buscar comida, escarban entre la nieve. Pueden comer la corteza de árboles y ramitas. En primavera, **mudan** su denso pelaje.

Fast Facts/Datos básicos

Height/ Altura	about 5 feet (2 meters) at the shoulder/ unos 5 pies (2 metros) en la cruz
Length/ Longitud	about 8 feet (3 meters) nose to tail/ unos 8 pies (3 metros) de nariz a cola
Weight/ Peso	Males: about 700 pounds (318 kilograms)/ Machos: unas 700 libras (318 kilogramos) Females: about 500 pounds (227 kilograms)/ Hembras: unas 500 libras (227 kilogramos)
Diet/ Dieta	grasses, shrubs, tree bark, and twigs/ pasto, arbustos, corteza de árboles y ramitas
Average life span/ Promedio de vida	up to 12 years/ hasta 12 años

Glossary/Glosario

antlers: the branched horns of animals in the deer family

calf: a baby elk

herd: a large group of elk or other animals

hooves: hard coverings on animals' feet

molt: to shed hair, skin, horn, or feathers

- - - - - - - - - - - - - - - - - - - -

astas: cuernos de algunos animales

cervatillo: cría de uapití y de otros venados

manada: grupo grande de uapitíes y de otros animales

mudar: perder pelo, piel, cuernos o plumas

pezuñas: recubrimientos duros de las patas de ciertos animales

For More Information/Más información

Books/Libros

Elk. Northern Trek (series). Scott Wrobel (Smart Apple Media, 2004)

I Live in the Mountains/Vivo en las montañas. Where I Live (series). Gini Holland (Gareth Stevens, 2004)

Web Sites/Páginas web

Elk/Uapitíes

animals.nationalgeographic.com/animals/mammals/elk.html
Watch a video of elk making their "bugling" call./Vean un video de los uapitíes emitiendo su llamada.

Elk/Uapitíes

www.eparks.org/wildlife_protection/wildlife_facts/elk.asp
Find out where you can see elk in the wild./Averigüen dónde encontrar uapitíes en libertad.

Publisher's note to educators and parents: Our editors have carefully reviewed these web sites to ensure that they are suitable for children. Many web sites change frequently, however, and we cannot guarantee that a site's future contents will continue to meet our high standards of quality and educational value. Be advised that children should be closely supervised whenever they access the Internet.

Nota de la editorial a los padres y educadores: Nuestros editores han revisado con cuidado las páginas web para asegurarse de que son apropiadas para niños. Sin embargo, muchas páginas web cambian con frecuencia, y no podemos garantizar que sus contenidos futuros sigan conservando nuestros elevados estándares de calidad y de interés educativo. Tengan en cuenta que los niños deben ser supervisados atentamente siempre que accedan a Internet.

Index/Índice

About the Author

JoAnn Early Macken is the author of two rhyming picture books, *Sing-Along Song* and *Cats on Judy*, and more than 80 nonfiction books for children. Her poems have appeared in several children's magazines. She lives in Wisconsin with her husband and their two sons.

- - - - - - - - - - - - - -

Información sobre la autora

JoAnn Early Macken ha escrito dos libros de rimas con ilustraciones, *Sing-Along Song* y *Cats on Judy*, y más de ochenta libros de no ficción para niños. Sus poemas han sido publicados en varias revistas infantiles. Vive en Wisconsin con su esposo y sus dos hijos.